Pokémon

BLACK & WHITE

EMOLGA MAKES MISCHIEF

Based on the episode "Emolga and the New Volt Switch!"

by Simcha Whitehill

ISBN 978-0-545-38073-7

12 11 10 9 8 7 6 5 4   12 13 14 15 16 17/0

Designed by Cheung Tai
Printed in the U.S.A.
First printing, January 2012

40

SCHOLASTIC INC.

| New York | Toronto | London | Auckland |
| Sydney | Mexico City | New Delhi | Hong Kong |

It was a bright and sunny day. Ash, Cilan, Iris, and their new friend Bianca were walking through the woods. They were on their way to Nimbasa City.

"Way to go catching Emolga, Iris!" Ash said. Iris had just captured the wild Electric- and Flying-type.

"Let's have a battle between Emolga and my Pignite," said Bianca.

"Okay! I accept your challenge," said Iris. She took Emolga out.

"It's so cute!" Bianca squealed.

"Emolga, use Hidden Power," said Iris.

Pignite fired up Heat Crash.
Emolga countered with Attract.
Instantly, Pignite was surrounded by hearts. Emolga had charmed it!
   "Pigniiiiite," it sighed. It stared at Emolga with hearts in its eyes.

"Pignite, return!" cried Bianca.

"Good battle strategy, Iris!" cheered Cilan.

"My next Pokémon is Minccino," said Bianca. She told Minccino to use Tickle.

"*Emo emo,*" Emolga giggled.

"Quick, Emolga, use Hidden Power!" Iris shouted.

Emolga let out a burst of light. But it also snuck in a Volt Switch. Emolga disappeared from the battle and another of Iris's Pokémon took its place!

"*Excadrill!*" cried Iris's Ground- and Steel-type. It landed with a thud.

"Huh?" Iris said. Emolga had used Volt Switch to escape the battle. It had put Excadrill in its place!

Emolga giggled at its trick. Bianca and Iris had to laugh, too.

"Emolga, what's the point of having this battle if you're going to use Volt Switch?" Iris asked. "Since we're doing this for practice, I hope you'll do what I ask you to."

Emolga burst into tears.

"Now you made Emolga cry!" exclaimed Ash.

"Emolga! Please stop crying," Iris pleaded.

Iris was worried about Emolga. It just didn't seem to want to battle.

"Building trust between Trainer and Pokémon is what training is all about," Cilan said.

"You have to be friends first," Ash agreed.

"A Pokémon battle can be fun if you put your heart into it, Emolga!" Iris told her Pokémon. "What do you say we give this rematch with Pignite one more try?"

Emolga shrugged. It didn't seem to care about Iris or the battle.

But Iris was determined to continue.
She told Emolga to use Hidden Power.
The little Pokémon obeyed. Then it
used Volt Switch to disappear again!
"Emolga, where did you go?" Iris
worried.

Iris searched the woods for Emolga. She found it sleeping in a tree.

"Emolga, come down here this instant!" Iris yelled.

But Emolga ignored her. So Ash's Snivy stepped in and used Vine Whip to carry it down.

"Why don't we take a food break?"
Cilan suggested.

Cilan handed a piece of fruit to
each Pokémon. But one piece wasn't
enough for Emolga. It used Attract
to get Tepig, Oshawott, Swadloon,
and Scraggy to hand over their
lunches.

When Emolga's spell wore off, the other Pokémon didn't know what had happened to their food. And they were very hungry! The four Pokémon started to fight.

"*Pikachuuuu!*" Pikachu yelped. It broke up the scuffle with a mighty Thunderbolt.

"Hey, what's going on here?" Ash asked.

"I think they're mad because someone stole their food," Cilan said.

"Who would do that?" asked Iris.

Snivy pointed to Emolga. Ash's Pokémon had seen the whole thing, and it wasn't fooled a bit.

"Just a minute!" cried Iris. "Emolga wouldn't do an awful thing like that. Would you, Emolga?"

"*Emo emo!*" Emolga cried. Tears rolled down its face.

"See?" said Iris.

"Guess you're right. Sorry!" said Ash.

Lunch was over, and the Trainers were ready to go. Until...

"I feel a little sleepy!" Ash said, yawning.

While the four Trainers took a nap under a big tree, Emolga woke up and sneaked into the woods. Oshawott and Axew decided to follow it.

Emolga was still hungry. It found a tree full of fruit in the forest. But a pack of wild Watchog was in the tree, and they didn't want to share.

Just then, Axew and Oshawott came down the path. Emolga decided to trick them. It told them that the Watchog had stolen the fruit from it.

"*Osha!*" Ash's Water-type Pokémon was angry. So Oshawott used its scalchop to slice some fruit off the tree for Emolga.

The three Watchog didn't like that one bit. They came after Oshawott. But they missed and slammed into a big tree. Ouch!

The loud noise woke a wild Simisear. It stormed over and fired a fierce Flamethrower. The Watchog were terrified. They ran away.

Oshawott tried to defend its friends. But Simisear knocked it against a tree. Axew didn't know what to do.

As for Emolga, it bit into a fruit like it had nothing to do with all this trouble.

The giant Simisear stomped up to Emolga. The little Pokémon finished its fruit and threw the core right at Simisear's nose.

"*Emo emo!*" Emolga laughed.

That made Simisear really angry. The big red Pokémon took a couple of swings at Emolga. But the fast Electric- and Flying-type dodged the Fire-type's fists.

"*Emo emo!*" cried Emolga, laughing again.

Now Simisear was boiling mad! It wound up a big punch to hit Emolga and Axew.

That's when Snivy came to the rescue! It had secretly followed Axew and Oshawott into the woods. It stopped Simisear with Vine Whip.

"*Simiseaaaaaaaar!*" the wild Pokémon shouted, firing Flamethrower.

Emolga tried to run away from the fight. But Snivy used Vine Whip to drag it back. This time, Emolga had to clean up its own mess!

Simisear shot another fiery
Flamethrower. Snivy protected its
friends with Leaf Blade. But it could
not avoid Simisear's Fire Punch. *Pow!*
"*Snivy!*" the little Grass-type cried
in pain.

Just then, Iris, Ash, Bianca, and
Cilan found the Pokémon in trouble.
"There they are!" cried Ash.
"Quick, Emolga!" Iris called.
"Help everyone out!"

Emolga looked around. The other
Pokémon were in big trouble! And
it was all Emolga's fault. The little
Pokémon realized it had to do
something.

So Emolga bravely jumped into the
battle. It flew around Simisear and
blasted it with Hidden Power.

Simisear tried to fire back with Flamethrower, but super fast Snivy tripped it with Vine Whip.

Simisear's Flamethrower shot into the cliffs above and broke off a huge rock. The boulder was headed right for Simisear's head!

"Simisear!" it cried out for help.

Emolga and Snivy were ready!
Emolga used Hidden Power to break
up the rock. Then Snivy used Leaf
Storm to blow the fragments away.

"Snivy, you were great!" Ash said.

"You, too, Emolga!" cheered Iris.

"Sim simisear," said the big
Pokémon, thanking them.

Iris was bursting with pride for her Pokémon.

Emolga smiled. It was proud of itself too. It picked up the last fruit on the ground and handed it to its new friends, Axew and Snivy.

"Emo emolga," it said, thanking Snivy for its help.

Snivy cut the fruit into three pieces so they could all enjoy the snack.

"It appears those three are now friends!" Cilan declared.

Emolga smiled. From now on, it would be there for its buddies.